MOMologues 3:
The Final Push

by Lisa Rafferty,
Stefanie Cloutier
and Sheila Eppolito

A SAMUEL FRENCH ACTING EDITION

SAMUELFRENCH.COM
SAMUELFRENCH-LONDON.CO.UK

FOR PRODUCTION ENQUIRIES

UNITED STATES AND CANADA
Info@SamuelFrench.com
1-866-598-8449

UNITED KINGDOM AND EUROPE
Plays@SamuelFrench-London.co.uk
020-7255-4302

Each title is subject to availability from Samuel French, depending upon country of performance. Please be aware that *MOMOLOGUES 3: THE FINAL PUSH* may not be licensed by Samuel French in your territory. Professional and amateur producers should contact the nearest Samuel French office or licensing partner to verify availability.

MOMOLOGUES 3: THE FINAL PUSH premiered at the Company Theatre in Norwell, Massachusetts in a benefit performance for Operation: Military Kids on May 16, 2012. It was directed by Lisa Rafferty and featured cast members Paula Markowicz, Erica McDermott, Melissa McMeekin and Ilyse Robbins.

CHARACTERS

ANN

JANE

TINA

WENDY

*MOMologues 3 is dedicated to our children:
without them, there would be no comedy.*

ACT ONE

TINA. Middle school and high school are payback time. It's when your kids do to *you* what *you* did to your mom and dad. Sweet vindication for grandparents. Think about it. Of course we were never *bad,* never talked to *our parents that way,* right? Right.

JANE. Between being peri-menopausal and my daughters being PMSy, and my son's whatevers kicking in, big time, wow - it's like Grand Central Hormones at my house. The Hormone Super Bowl. Hormones R Us. The World Series of Hormones. Ready for our own reality show and it's not going to be pretty.

WEN. Some people say that today's kids have an exaggerated sense of entitlement and a ridiculous level of self-involvement...I would be one of those people and I would be talking about my own children.

ANN. I am so done with elementary school. My oldest is in high school, my youngest still has a year to go till he reaches middle school, but I am totally over the elementary school experience. I'm done with the Cookie Walk, the Spelling Bee, the Carnival Fundraiser. I've lost interest in the Hobby Fair, the Ice Cream Social and the Turkey Trot. Family Fun Night? I don't think so. And when I do show up, the parents all look so much younger: they're bouncing babies on their hips, pulling sippy cups out of purses, handing baggies of goldfish to tiny people. I'm ready to put it all behind me, I can't begin to tell you.

****

TINA. My daughter comes home after her first club meeting at the High School – Math Club, God help me. We're chatting about her day and the club and I'm actually thinking – this is great – we're communicating.

Excellent. Then she says: "Do you know about bases? Matt's friend was telling me about bases." Oh shit. Who is Matt's friend? The little pervert. I'll wring his neck. She's 14 for God's sake. Here we go. And then she says, "I can't really describe it to you, so let me draw it." Whoa. Drawing it??? What is going on here? What the hell is going on in Math Club?? So she looks down at the paper and says 'So you take the number 65, and there is a difference between numbers and numerals, and everything is not a base of ten…' and it dawns on me – the bases she is talking about - binary numbers. That's it. What the hell?

JANE. My daughter is in high school. *High. School.* That cannot be. I mean, I'm just barely out of high school myself…Okay, barely three decades ago, but still! I simply cannot be *that old* and neither can she. She's my little girl. She's not high school age. High school age means boyfriends and a drivers license and the young adult section at the library and babysitting little kids. And navigating stereotypes and gender issues, and trying new and possibly illegal things, and field trips to other states or countries without me. *(Big breath.)* She CAN'T be that old. *I* can't be that old. And yet… here we both are. And the way I know this is she is wearing my same shoe size. We are interchangeable with shoes. That has to be the unofficial milestone of your daughter coming of age. When you and she are both size 8's.

WEN. I already started with 'The Last' everything. Just had my last elementary Back to School night – my third kid, my *twentieth* Back to School night, we whipped through in about 12 minutes flat. 'So nice to meet you, what a great room, oh is this your desk, Buddy? Here are the room responsibilities, excellent – I see you are the paper passer outer this week. Your desk looks great. Okay, let's go through and meet your other teachers and we're done! SO nice to meet you. Isn't this all exciting? Well gotta go. Bye bye!' And now that my oldest is in high school we are doing all The Lasts there too – her last time getting on a bus, her last time first day of school, my last time making lunch for her, never mind what's going to happen senior year – no, no NOT READY. Not ready for all those firsts – you know, the firsts that we all did when we were teenagers. NOT READY!

****

ANN. Okay, when did Halloween costumes become Hoochy Mama porn get ups?

TINA. I know, seriously. My daughter is nine. Wants to be a witch. But the witches all look like Elvira, Mistress of Foreplay. Black satin bustier, thong-sized little pants. What's next, a free dildo-shaped flashlight for safe trick or treating?

ANN. And the COST of the kiddie porn…they're made in Malaysia of material that'd go up in flames in a MINUTE…and yet we're supposed to cough up $30.

TINA. When I was a kid, we'd wear our dads' old suits, use a burned wine cork to mess up our faces, and call ourselves "Bums." Imagine the PC police if you showed up for a Halloween party as a bum!

ANN. What happened to a cut up sheet and you're a ghost? When did disposable income become involved? And what's the cut-off, age-wise? My neighbor's rich little pothead 17 year old rang my bell last year. No costume, just glazed eyes and a big case of the munchies. I took pity and gave him some Skittles and three Reese's cups.

TINA. Last year, three kids ring my bell, dressed as Ninjas or Al Qaeda operatives or something. So I feign interest, and give them individual microwave popcorn bags. And one little shit puts up a fuss! "What's this? We're supposed to get CANDY!" he says.

ANN. What'd you say?

TINA. I launched into a lecture about how it's trick or TREAT. And popcorn is a TREAT. And, P.S., he should say thank you, no matter WHAT he gets. I'm sure I sounded like an 80 year old bitch, but seriously. Who's raising these little turds?

ANN. I remember when my youngest daughter was in kindergarten. She went as Spongebob. Cute as hell. Anyhow, there's a celebration of Halloween at school.

TINA. Sure, an acceptable holiday to celebrate in school.

ANN. And so I drag my butt there. But I'm a little late. I get there, and another mom asks me which kid is mine. I tell her she's Mr. Squarepants. She says, "Oh! I was wondering who her mom was!" So I figure it's because she's so cute....

TINA. Oh no...

ANN. But she tells me that before I came, the teacher was describing the various stations set up for the big celebration, you know, the paper-bag-scarecrow stuffing center, the decorate-a-gourd-with sprinkly-shit-station, and my daughter pipes up, AS the teacher is talking, and says, "Blah, blah, blah."

TINA. Kid after my own heart.

ANN. Yeah, proud mother I am – my kid is the wiseass in class. Where does she get that do you think?

TINA. Well...

ANN. Don't answer that...

****

JANE. Thanksgiving is my favorite holiday in some ways. No pressure on presents to buy, we usually stay local, we don't have to cram in some social or religious event into the day, the week, it's all about food, football, family and friends. What could be wrong with that? Wonderful. After all, it's a day to give thanks. Count our blessings. And who better – *who better?* – to do that than three teenage children. I ask you. *Is there any group on God's green earth that is more thankful, more filled with gratitude and love than teenagers?* I think not... Think about it. These are kids who know how to say, 'please, mom, can you drive me to my friend's house – at your convenience? 'Thanks, for the ride, Mom, you are the best.' 'How was my day at school? How thoughtful of you to ask. Let me tell you all about it.' Aren't all kids just like this? Mine are. Oh wait. I went to the alternative universe for a minute there. SO NOT my reality. In fact, over the door of MY house it says, 'Welcome to the Land of Surly, Grumpy and Secretive.' It's like 3 of the Dwarfs. The others are Sulky, Moody, Fresh, and Spoiled. It's all part of the ever-continuing learning curve of being a parent. There is *What You Dreamed It Would Be Like* and *What Is.* Waaaaaaay Apart. It's like when you thought you would never drive a minivan, and yet, there you were, three car seats in the back, Barney on a CD, goldfish crumbs everywhere, ready to scream. Or you envisioned your children as being fabulous, healthy eaters and instead you're undermining your most sacred ethics by being a short order cook for three different kids each night. Having three kids between the ages of 13 – 16 is like Field of Hopes and Dreams Crushed. You know it will pass – everyone tells you it will get better – but you just know: This is What Being a Parent Is. This is what separates the men from the boys. Where the rubber hits the road. Where the tough get going. Accept each new reality of your family life and try hard not to get bitter… So, yeah, I love Thanksgiving. I truly will be giving thanks and counting my blessings and I try *not to do it in an ironic way.* Promise. And I know that deep, deep, DEEP down, my kids will be grateful too. Bless their hearts.

****

ANN. The holiday season is a time when the whole mom thing kicks up a notch. The list just goes on and on.

WEN. Shopping, shopping, shopping – without having to re-mortgage the house.

TINA. Buying cards

ANN. Taking the Christmas photo.

JANE. Yeah, the attempt to capture the happy family photo for the holiday cards… C'mon stay still, STAY STILL, look at the camera, LOOK AT THE CAMERA, smile, smile, SMILE DAMMIT. STOP FOOLING AROUND YOU GUYS! SAY CHEESE, HEY NO RABBIT EARS BEHIND YOUR BROTHER'S HEAD! Hide that bra strap! Candy all around for those who cooperate. For those who don't, just hand over the cell phone now. Okay, two more. Pretend you're happy.

TINA. Writing the cards.

JANE. Mailing the cards.

ANN. Helping out at church.

WEN. Helping out at school.

JANE. Mall purgatory.

ANN. Black Friday.

WEN. Cyber Monday.

ANN. Arguing over which tree.

TINA. Hauling out the decorations.

JANE. Untangling the clusterfuck of outside lights.

ANN. Whoa – hostility there!

JANE. Tis the season.

TINA. Forced family fun.

ANN. Booking flights.

WEN. Pre-flight laundry.

ANN. Preparing for houseguests.

TINA. Making Christmas dinner.

WEN. Eating Chinese.

TINA. Wait… What?

WEN. On Christmas. For some of us. Then a movie.

JANE. Hosting parties.

ANN. Potluck holiday brunch.

WEN. Avoiding Santa.

TINA. Secret Santa.

JANE. Fake Santas.

ANN. Endless, nonstop holiday song assault.

JANE. Yankee fucking swap.

TINA. Last minute panic.

WEN. You know what we really need to do is…

ANN. Yes, absolutely!

ALL. "LET IT GO, LET IT GO, LET IT GO…" *(to the tune of "Let It Snow")**

TINA. The madness needs to stop.

ANN. Even if some of it is actually great and wonderful.

JANE. Shopping online has been helpful and life changing.

ANN. The decorations are still magical. Love driving around with the kids – even at this age – to see them.

JANE. And Christmas morning is still…mostly…awesome. Except for the ingratitude and attitude.

ANN. No – come back to the light! Don't stay in the dark side.

WEN. And speaking of lights – Hanukkah can be fun. Except for the latkes. And the scale the next day.

JANE. Okay, let's just leave it at that. Just don't get me started on things like the annual year in review Holiday card…

****

TINA. So the thing that drives me insane at Christmas is the family update form letter. Who are these people? They can't be the same flawed, grumpy, overworked and overwhelmed friends I know the rest of the year. And I really could give a crap about their family's accomplishments. I mean that with love, of course. I sit there and as I read the letter in my head I'm writing the subtext: "…and Jake was accepted on the pinochle team for gifted children in our homeschooling socialization circle! We couldn't be more proud!" They're like a fucking cult. A gifted fucking cult. "… meanwhile, Sue and Ned have expanded their career

---

*Please see Music Use Note on page 3

horizons to better align with their personal growth goals." Shorthand for FI-RED. Loving the third person reference. "Sue and Ned have expanded".... Did they hire a ghostwriter on this project? Not a chance! Who makes a personal growth goal anyhow for shit's sake. The homeschooling gifted pinochle enthusiast careerseekers, apparently. But who cares? I mean, who the fuck CARES? Why do people send these letters? To tell us how fucking busy they are? How fulfilling their scrapbooking weekend was? Who are these freaks? "...Sally began menstruating" "Tyler began masturbating...Trevor enjoyed his first scotch after turning 21 on a foxhunting trip with his stepdad!" ... This the same kid who barfed the Crème de Menthe through the screen door at his sister's Red Tent womanhood celebration? Yup ...one in the same. What's next? An update on their colorectal performance? "Carolyn's colon has never been cleaner, thanks to her devotion to a high-fiber vegan diet." I swear I'd welcome one that said, "We're doing the best we can. Our kids are finding their way, and we're trying to survive the bumps along the way. A little holiday humility, you know? Ho Ho Ho and a happy holidays to all!

****

JANE. You know how bullying is such a big issue? Well, what no one tells you is: American teenagers are capable of being the biggest bullies of all – to their parents.

ANN. You're not kidding. I consider myself to be a strong, independent woman. But my kids can reduce me to tears in a heartbeat.

WEN. I cower in my bedroom, afraid to come out sometimes.

JANE. How about when you brace yourself to ask something of the little ungrateful wretches?

ANN. Remind them to pick their crap up, for instance?

WEN. Let you know more than 5 minutes ahead of time if they need a ride?

JANE. How about the inevitable all-caps text: 'WHERE ARE YOU? I'M WAITING!'

ANN. It's like being a personal assistant to a big star. I DEMAND GREEN M&M'S AND FIJI WATER – AND PICK UP MY DRY CLEANING.

WEN. And why is every request you make of them considered 'yelling?'

JANE. *(in a nice voice)* Can you please empty the dishwasher?

ANN. WHY ARE YOU YELLING AT ME LIKE THAT?

WEN. Yeah, exactly.

JANE. Oh, you'll KNOW when I'm yelling. BECAUSE IT WILL SOUND LIKE THIS!

ANN. And I love when I do laundry, and I've done all the sorting and folding and I bring it up for them to put away, and I get the big sigh…

WEN. Yeah, like it's SO HARD to put it away in the drawer.

JANE. Well, if your son is anything like mine, there's no difference between clean and dirty laundry – it just all goes into the hamper to be washed over and over.

ANN. I know but the way my son's clothes smell, they need to be washed over and over…

JANE. Right? Sometimes I hold my breath when I walk into his room…

WEN. That's how my daughter 'cleans' her room – just takes everything, whether it's dirty or not, and dumps it into the laundry basket. I can't tell you how often I wash clean clothes.

ANN. Everything you ask is a huge imposition.

WEN. I don't even bother. I'd rather be a martyr. It helps with the guilt.

JANE. They are seemingly incapable of the most basic things. At eight my daughter was helping me cook, now it's like "Mom, can you make me my cereal?' Seriously?

ANN. I know the whole "I can do it by MYSELF" thing on the one hand, on the other, "What medicine should I take?"

WEN. How are they going to live on their own at college? Oy.

JANE. I don't know but will I make it to then? It's all you can do sometimes to last until they go to school. It's like dreading snow days – oh no, THE HORROR!

WEN. My kids wake up to the sound of me cursing and swearing. I'm watching the TV crawl, praying and praying that my superintendent manned up and kept the damn schools open.

ANN. Scrambling for kid coverage so I can get to work, or worse, calling work to say I can't come in. Kids assaulting me to find their snow boots, gloves, make hot chocolate, pull down the sleds from the top of the garage…yeah, relaxing.

JANE. It's just a huge relief to go to work sometimes – who knew a job could be such an escape?

WEN. It's like I love being with my hypothetical kids. The kids I know and love in my mind. My reality kids – not so much right now.

JANE. Thank God for my dog. No parent of teenagers should be without a dog. On some days – many days – she is the only one that loves me, for me. And she's a good listener.

WEN. True, and it works both ways. The kids go to our dog too, when they need love and can't – or won't – get it from me.

ANN. Yes, the only benign presence in our house. On all sides. It's like pets are the Switzerland of creatures.

WEN. Three teenagers, 1 dog – I need to find another pet…

****

TINA. For New Year's resolutions, other people vow to quit smoking, or lose 10 pounds or pay bills on time. But I'm a mom, a flawed, imperfect, inconsistent, over thinking mess – and that's on the good days. So my

New Year's resolutions are like: *Nag less, hug more.* Improve the kids eating habits – healthy snacks! Go with the flow more – lighten up, Francis! You know, all the same resolve you start off with every morning, but by nightfall it's all gone to hell - gone is the patience, the nurturing, the modeling the good behavior. It's like you start out all "yes, sweetheart, what is it?" and by 6:00 p.m. it's "I'll give you something to cry about." So, yeah, suffice to say, my New Year's resolution is to be Morning Mom all day. Like that's ever going to happen...

WEN. I'm such a stickler for table manners. It's upbringing, it's genetic, it's my control freak thing going full throttle – who knows? Trying to get my kids to absorb and remember good manners at the table is the same mind numbing, brain hurting, daily grind that is so much of parenting, over and over and fucking over again. Sit up straight. Yes please or no thank you. Chew with your mouth closed. Don't talk with your mouth full!! Why does it have to be all of those every day? Every day! Three meals a day for weeks, months, years. It's getting so I can't get through a meal without being the *Horror Nag Mom from Hell*... So, it's dessert time and my daughter is maniacally slurping her ice cream in the bowl, like some possessed mad lunatic – and I hit the breaking point and I just lose it. STOP PLAYING WITH YOUR FOOD! JUST STOP IT! YOU ARE GOING INTO 5TH GRADE! YOU SHOULD KNOW BETTER! STOP PLAYING WITH YOUR FOOD! ANY FOOD! EVER! AAAAAGHHH!... And she is staring at me – spoon frozen mid air above the ice cream – looking shocked and hurt at my outburst. And now I'm thinking God, what has happened to me! I'm taking all the fun out of food!! I mean she is 10 years old – 10! And I'm so over the edge I can even let her slurp a little ice cream. What has happened to me? Do I not have a single shred of fun, of spontaneity, left? Must I annihilate my children's spontaneity too?

And then my next thought is, okay, I am fucking losing it. Extrapolating out my entire existence as a mother over one moment of parental anger over manners. Like no one has ever done that before. And sometimes it needs to be said... And then I just go to the sink and start doing dishes...

JANE. I've had bosses, college roommates and have known politicians that are manipulative, sneaky and calculating. But none, none compare to my daughter, who is a master of twisting my words and gaming the system. Cutting out the middle of brownies so she gets all the good part, taking the last bit of cereal, always wanting control of the clicker, bossing everyone around to get her own way, throwing my words back in my face with unceasing regularity. Using tactics to make the most jaded of lawyers would appreciate: the relentless cross examination, the evasive non answer, the power of tears, the insistent misdirection. It takes every ounce of strength I have to hold my own in these tug of wars. And you don't dare show weakness or you will be crushed. So you buck up, and assault her with the vast array of parenting techniques, using positive and negative reinforcement strategies like nobody's business. And somewhere down inside you are a little bit proud, a little bit glad, because she has what it takes to get by in the cold, cruel world. She'll have the wherewithal to hold her own against people who behave not unlike she behaved toward her parents. And, no question, she'll make a great attorney...

ANN. Do you remember birthday parties?? The eighteen screaming children, the piñata filled with candy, the craft activity designed for maximum mess, the party favors full of sugar. And lots of crying. The birthday kid, the birthday guests, the birthday parents... The utter exhaustion at the end of the two hour ordeal. Well, here's the good news. I just threw one for my 14 year old, and it was the exact opposite experience. My daughter planned almost the whole thing, from the invitations to the activity to the food. I was only necessary as the bank account and food server; otherwise, I was virtually invisible, and oh so superfluous, as far as the guests were concerned. I overheard everything they said, but realized my comments were of absolutely no interest to them. They didn't want my opinions on the latest teen movie, or my expertise on getting through high school. They completely entertained themselves, then decorated their own cupcakes. Even the present opening did not require my presence: no keeping track of who gave what for the future thank you card, and certainly no oohing and ahing over the gifts: they only wanted to hear from their own bad selves. They ate every morsel of food I put in front of them, and then some. I actually sat in the other room and read, when I wasn't required to bring out more food. So, it doesn't all get harder as they get older. Some things, just some things, get easier!

****

JANE. So, I know we can all be good moms at times. But there are certain areas where I have *failed as a mother*. For instance, food. You know, vegetables. Three kids, no vegetables among them. *And my daughter is a vegetarian.* Or a pastaterian as we call her. C'mon help me out here, other failure areas?

ANN. Sleeping. They sleep fine, it's the going to bed part that is an excruciating exercise for both parties. The endless negotiation, the bargaining, or just plain ignoring. Brutal.

WEN. Chores. My kids don't do any.

TINA. I've got the chores thing down. They hate me for it, but too bad. Healthy eating? It's not terrible, I guess, but it's not great either.

TINA. We are all too hard on ourselves.

WEN. We all have those things that we are good at and the things we will never, ever be. I will never, ever be the kind of mom who never yells. Always wanted to be that mom, know those moms, SO NOT that mom. I'm a yeller. Sometimes it seems the only way to get through. But then I get mad at them when they yell at me – or at each other.

JANE. Do as I say, not as I do. I have been more or less living in fear of when my kids start to ask my husband and me about our own sordid teenage and college years. Good Lord, I've read all the articles and advice books there are on this subject and my gut reaction is LIE. LIE, LIE, LIE. There's just no way to not sound completely two faced – oh no, honey, it was different in our day – when we were doing bong hits and guzzling beer in fraternity basements – DIFFERENT.

TINA. I am a friggin hounddog. Sniff test the hands for pot…check breath for booze. And I get right into their faces, checking for fear or paranoia. If they're minty fresh and hungry, be very afraid.

ANN. Well, my parenting fail is in the listening department. I KNOW we're supposed to just drop everything and be all ears WHENEVER our teens choose to talk to us, but why does it always have to be right as I want to drop exhausted into bed? I mean, I THINK I'm just popping my head in to say goodnight, and right then is when she wants to talk about the exam she wished she'd prepared better for, or why her friend is avoiding her in the halls… I mean, really, couldn't we have this conversation when my brain hasn't already shut down for the night?

WEN. Oh, and can I just say something about the teen tantrums? Man the terrible twos have got NOTHIN on them! At least when they're small you can either pick them up and move them, or walk around them. But at this age, they follow you around, or stomp those size 10 feet all the way to their rooms…pretty damn ugly.

ANN. Look, it's just damned if you do, damned if you don't. Like being the President but without the perks.

TINA. If you accept that you can't win, it's better. Try to be noble in your failure. There is good in all our parenting… Somewhere.

WEN. Now if we can just get a little gratitude coming our way for the good things we do.

JANE. Not going to happen.

ANN. In fact, I'm grout.

WEN. What?? What are you talking about?

ANN. Grout – you know, the stuff that goes between the tiles, holding them in place?

TINA. Ah, yes, the stuff no one ever notices…

ANN. Unless, of course, it's not there and the tiles pop up and go missing. Then everyone's all "these tiles need to be fixed"; it's never "oh, let's get more of that awesome grout!"

JANE. Right, because they're all paying attention to the beautiful tile; everyone thinks the tiles are SO important.

ANN. Exactly. But it's the grout that does all the dirty work, like the food shopping…

WEN. And putting it all away while the kids sit on the couch staring at their iPhone…

JANE. The laundry, Good Lord, the laundry, relentless, unceasing day after day…

TINA. The sweeping, cleaning, organizing, throwing away

WEN. Who knew so much of motherhood would be about throwing away? School papers, art work, progress reports, the grout makes those weighty decisions everyday.

ANN. Leaving work to drive to hockey rink, to dance, to the orthodontist, to the SAT prep class…

TINA. To school when they miss the bus because they just weren't paying attention to the time even though I give them time checks like every three minutes…

WEN. And then the ridiculous trips back to school with the important project they FORGOT to pack in their backpacks. My kids know the rule: I'll do that three times and then that's it. They are outa luck after that.

ANN. Well, one of these days, THIS grout is going to wear out. And then they'll just have to figure out how to make those tiles stick together on their own. No more walking all over me, the ungrateful creatures that they are.

TINA. Amen, sister!

ANN. THIS grout will be quietly chuckling while she sips her fruity drink with the little umbrella on a white sandy beach somewhere really, really warm… Ah, a girl can dream, can't she?

WEN. Sad thing is we will actually miss all of it when they are gone. But with any luck, we'll remember all the good instead of the failures.

TINA. Yeah, like that's going to happen…

****

ANN. I have a confession to make: I am a barely adequate mother. Really. Now, I know there will be some who protest that, people who think they've seen me parent my children and feel they know enough to vigorously defend me, but I know better. When they were tiny and needy, I found them overwhelming, with their inability to tell me exactly what they needed from me. I found it exhausting to try to interpret their cries, their hurt looks, their meltdowns at inappropriate times. There were times when I would sit on the side of my bed, crying, and look heavenward and plead, I am not the right mother for this, you need to make it stop, I can't do this. I can't do this. And I loved them, really, but it just took so much EFFORT, you know? I just wanted it to not be so hard. For me. Because plenty of other people seemed to make it look – well, easier, at least. Now of course they're much older, it's not that same overwhelming panic, that sense of being completely incapable of being a good-enough parent. And I was thinking back to those days, and thinking about how much easier it is for me now – not that I'm magically a better mother, but realizing that I've definitely improved. And I realize it's because of them: they made me change the way I parent. They, with their refusing to just lie down and do what I expected, forced me to try new things, sometimes outlandish things, sometimes things no other parent might ever do. And in doing those things, I've learned to become the very specific parent they, my own children, need. I'm still far, far less than perfect, and I still have a long, long way to go. But I know I'm a better person, precisely BECAUSE of them. I'm a better mom. Despite my own bad self, they made me a better mom.

TINA. You know, before I had kids, I had a life – a full life, with a job and friends and activities even. I can't remember exactly WHAT those activities were, but I remember being very busy. A rich, full life. And then I had kids. And I have to say, I was a little resentful at times of all that I had to give up that was just for ME. Now I was doing Mommy and me classes, and going to toddler gym, and hanging with other moms. And that morphed into soccer games and ballet classes and girl scouts and myriad other activities that I didn't necessarily choose, but that my kids begged to be a part of. Wow. And my days were filled, but with activities for other people, not me. But I was very busy. And now those kids are becoming teenagers, and their activities don't necessarily include me. They don't want me hanging around while they bond with their friends. Oh, they still need me to drive them around, but they don't want me horning in on their conversations. I still think I'm young and cool and hip, but they want their own lives, and they see me as "the mom". So I can see it coming: the day they can drive themselves to all their stuff and then I'm not even needed for the car pool. And I can't eavesdrop on their conversations anymore. I guess then I'll have time for my own activities, ones that I choose just for me. I just wish I could remember what they were…

WEN. After watching your kids try so many different things as they go through elementary school and middle school – some soccer, a little lacrosse, chorus, art club, Little League and Boy Scouts, jazz, tap and ballet – it's fascinating to see what they really hang their hats on in high school. Your son's budding career as a second baseman? Gone. In it's place – ski team. Your daughter's 10 years of dance? Not so much. More like photography class and babysitting. All those years going to boy scout meetings? Now it's Anime and robotics. Sure, some things stay as a continued passion – in fact they become the abiding passion – all hockey, all the time. Theater, theater and more theater. Student government every year. As it happens, you realize that they are evolving into their own true selves – not following your guidance or interests – but pushing back on what they want to try, what they want to do. And while you have always been bursting with pride at all they accomplish, somehow this is even more special because it comes from deep inside of them, not from outside influence. And you watch, and wonder, and are amazed. At the people they have become. At the glimpse of where there are going. At the miracle that they are, every day, even when they are driving you crazy. And you are so, so grateful for all of it.

JANE. I always wanted my family to be the kind that would hug and love each other in a really great way. It wasn't like that for me growing up, but I always envied that in other families. Sure, when the kids were little it worked that way. But as they got older, they pulled away, figuratively and literally. Even though I wanted hold them and kiss them every day, it just didn't happen. So I hold them and love them in my mind instead. As I am driving them around, or watching them in a concert or run around a soccer field, or sit across the dinner table from me. I send out love. Even when they are being nasty, even when they are being difficult…I say it too, even when the timing seems awkward, when it only comes back in that uniquely reluctant teenage way. And sometimes there are still magic moments – when my son and I snuggle on the couch as we watch something on TV or when we can talk and laugh when

I come in to say goodnight, or when my daughter is not feeling well, and still needs TLC from me or when my oldest daughter, the one who is pulling away as she gets ready for college, spontaneously hugs me and tells me she loves me. Magic. What we live for. So grateful for their wonderful, annoying, kind, selfish, smart, dumb, fascinating, obnoxious, insecure, amazing selves. So profoundly grateful that this is why I was put on this good Earth. And that's all that truly matters.

ACT TWO

JANE. Why is polite behavior totally gone? Must we regress back to the toddler years with the reminders? "I didn't hear 'please.'" "Did you mean 'Thank You, Mom'?" And can they flush the toilet *and* wash their hands? Is this too much to ask? What about sitting still at dinner? Never mind the complete disregard for where they leave their shoes, backpacks, coats, cleats, dirty socks, sweatshirts, dirty towels, laundry, etc. They want to be so grown up and independent on the one hand. On the other hand, every 8 year old I know beats my teenage children in the basic etiquette department. However, like all things that are infuriating at this stage, to the outside world my kids are absolute gems. Smart, polite, respectful, enthusiastic, funny and charming. You know what I'm talking about. But at our house? I think their IQ drops when they cross the threshold. Rudeness prevails, respect is an elusive quality, enthusiasm is non-existent, charming is Nowhere To Be Found, *although funny still pays a visit.* Thank God. They are all wicked funny. But manners? Not so much. Please tell me it gets better. I actually do know it will get better. How? Because, of course, I was the same annoying teenager to my parents. Somewhere in heaven, my mom is getting a good laugh. The good and the bad – it all comes around doesn't it?

ANN. I will be the first to tell you that I am not a baby person. I far prefer the little buggers once they can tell you what they want. But one thing I do miss from those early days is the smell of that newborn baby head. There's just nothing like it. And you just can't believe that the teen boy version of that little thing will someday smell like a cross between a wet dog and a sweaty ogre. Seriously, the stench can knock me over from five feet away; I have no idea how his friends stand anywhere near him. And it's not like he doesn't shower! Oh, no, he does that every single morning, sometimes twice in one day. And yet in no time at all he smells like something overripe and funky, something I would throw out without even touching if I found it in my fridge. We've had the hygiene talk, the don't-forget-to-use-soap-in-the-shower talk, and the 'yes you have to use deodorant every single day' talk, but somehow all that cleaning and deodorizing still can't stand up to active, sweaty boy. I know that this, too, shall pass: after all, I married someone who was once a ball-playing teen, and he smells just fine. So I guess I just have to wait it out – and buy some more air freshener for the house...

TINA. Ok, people, what's up with kid sports? And I'm not talking about the fact that they take over every weekend and force me to drive from one end of the state to the other in order to see each kid play some fraction of a game. I'm talking about using youth sports to groom mini athletes for – what? Bad knees and torn rotator cuffs? Seriously, I thought the whole point of signing up for Saturday morning soccer was for the camaraderie that comes from playing on a team, learning to be a good sport, and keeping busy so mommy doesn't have to occupy ALL her kids' time. But now we have club hockey, AAU baseball and star soccer, elite teams that seem to be year-round, running drills in the off-season and cramming in umpteen games a week once the season starts. And what are we training them FOR, anyway? Do we really expect them to become professional athletes? What's the point? Or have we become so hyper-competitive that even what was SUPPOSED to be fun, a change from the grueling academic world where kids could blow off a little steam and be kids, has now become no-holds-barred ramped up athletic training? Not every kid is going to be the best, the strongest, the hardest throwing; some of them are going to loll about the outfield, or warm the bench, or worse still, burn out before they're even through puberty. Me, I'd like my kids to play a sport they love and want to spend time doing, a sport that makes them work a little, gets them out to enjoy the sunshine. Oh, and maybe happens right after school, at a conveniently located field, where I don't have to drive them. Is it vacation time yet?

****

JANE. Okay girlfriends, our next trip is supposed to be to Disney. So is that a much needed mid-winter break or school holiday Hell?

ANN. What?

JANE. Seriously. Throngs of oily, sweating, desperate people, sucking on turkey legs, banging back Mickey corn dogs. Shoot me.

WEN. I love Disney! We go every single year! We're like the Fast Pass kings. Last year, we did Splash Mountain 17 times!

ANN. You say that like it's a good thing. C'mon did anyone hurl?

WEN. Nooooooo. In fact, we went right from Splash Mountain to Discovery Cove, where we hung out at the coolest beach and tube park.

JANE. Fake beach. Pretend waves. Make believe fun. Not an ocean for miles. Costs a small fortune.

WEN. What about rides and learning about places from all around the world? Have you been to Epcot?

ANN. Some geography lesson that is. Norway is next to Thailand. Lunch at the Morrocco Pavillion. Dinner at the Japan Pavillion.

WEN. We love it. We're obsessed, we map out every minute before we get there. We trade pins, color-coordinate our T-shirts, take photos with every character. My husband even wears his Goofy hat so we can find him.

JANE. Doesn't he feel like an asshole – a grown man – an ACCOUNTANT even – wearing dog ears in 110 degrees?

WEN. Okay, Debbie Downer. No – I think he feels like a Dad, having fun.

ANN. The happiest place on earth, I know.

JANE. No that we've got that settled, you know what's funny? When I'm mad at something my son or my daughters are doing – when I am in a snit about some part of their personality that is driving me nuts – I secretly think – 'he is just like his father.'

ANN. 'He is as lazy as his father…'

WEN. 'I can't believe she pulls that same passive aggressive shit that he does.'

JANE. I'm sure my husband is thinking the same thing. 'Oh great, another generation of neurotic women.'

ANN. 'Looks like the OCD got passed down after all.'

WEN. 'Cannot believe my son is listening to show tunes.'

JANE. Of course I do give credit where credit is due – good in math, likes to ski…

ANN. Plays guitar like a rock star.

WEN. And sometimes the credit or the blamegoes back to my mother or father – or his mother or father.

ANN. The poor kids. They can't be their own beautiful, wonderful, flawed selves.

JANE. They have to be burdened with decades of family history without even knowing it.

WEN. Only solace I have is that they'll do the same things to their kids.

JANE. I'm quite sure my grandchildren will only get the best parts of me…

****

TINA. My oldest daughter is going to Spain on a school exchange thing where she'll live with a family for 10 days. People I've never *seen*, let alone Googled. Seriously, I know it's a great chance for her – flying over the ocean, landing, getting off the plane with her friends, and hearing a whole different world. Smelling a new place, seeing new trees, shoes, all of it so different. So exciting. I still remember my first time. But she's really GOING. I'm not so much worried about the plane – it's more what happens when she DEplanes. Who shows up to pick her up? It's worrying me now – months too late – WHO ARE THESE PEOPLE? And what is the drinking age? IS there a drinking age? And do they have Rufis? How do you say Rufis in Spanish? Rufos? And what's the protection strategy for a Rufi.. never leave your drink anywhere, right? Well this kid is really, really smart, but also has a head full of stuff and sometimes she forgets things. Like a drink. How can I get her to remember to bring her drink to the bathroom? And what *is* she drinking anyhow? To calm myself down, I've begun playing tapes in my head where this happy, loving, hard working family comes along in their clean but modest station wagon with a sandwich for her in case she's hungry. They're so pleased to see her! They have planned a lovely fiesta with the 100 year old Abuela. Plaintains. Paella. Flan. Excellent. And then the channel changes in my head, and instead of the nice *family*, it's some over-cologned, misunderstood, hormonally tortured, beautiful Spanish boy — man, really, the brother in the family, and the only one free to pick her up in the middle of the day. Probably unemployed! And he catches a look at her, and sees my beautiful, beautiful baby. And starts the seduction plan right away. OH MY GOD! Okay, so it's probably not a family in a long, Buick wagon, and it's probably not going to be the horny young stud, either. What if it's an aging stud? Old guy, still tanned, used to be handsome. Maybe Ricardo Montalban? Is he Spanish? Is he even ALIVE? So we went to Kohl's yesterday to get her squared away for the trip – she was told to bring a dress, and heels, because they like to go to the disco in their town. THE DISCO? So we get her a cute dress – and I wisely suggest a cute *sweater* to go over it, in case she gets cold. Seriously –" just cover every inch of that beautiful body up" is what I want to say. I want to cover her in a fucking tarp. I can't handle it, I'm serious. We're headed from juniors over to shoes, and she says to me, "Hey mom? Can I get one of those strapless bras for the dress?" A STRAPLESS FUCKING BRA? Let me tell you this – the bras for 15 year olds are loaded up with like 4 pounds of molded memory foam boob material…so that EVERY kid who wears one looks like something off *The Bachelor*. But we find one that will work, and we're good. On the way to the checkout – I've got my Kohl's Cash and my 30% off everything coupon in hand – I see some cute necklaces on sale. I pick up one that says "daughter" on it. And I buy it. Not because I liked it, but because maybe it'll remind her of me if she's on the verge of something. And stop her cold. Or maybe Ricardo Montalban will squint his rheumy AARP eyes and see it, and it will remind him that she's someone's daughter, and he'll go away. It's a little too late to realize I've probably made the biggest mistake of my life. Willingly send her to a foreign country…at 15?! And pay for it? What was I THINKING?? Why didn't people STOP ME? I allowed it to happen, when I could have easily said NO. Too expensive, too something. I could have bought myself some more time. She still sleeps with a teddy bear for crying out loud. She's strong, and smart, and I trust her judgment. But no matter how smart she is…who knows a friggin' THING at 15? It's too late to turn back. She's going, she's leaving. Ready or not. There she goes.

ANN. I have a teenage daughter. I know what that means to most people: boy-craziness, dodging homework for Facebook, incessant texting – well, you know the drill. But here's the thing: my kid's not like that. I've got the "anti-teen." My kid not only doesn't text, she rarely even turns her phone on. She only uses Facebook to check out photos posted by friends – she doesn't write status updates or change her profile picture, or even comment on other people's posts. She has little interest in fashion or makeup, beyond wearing clothes that are comfortable and that match, and she spends her spare time perusing fish forums for information on stocking her aquarium. She's something of a homebody, likes to hang with her parents on a Saturday night, watching movies and snuggling up on the couch. Now, I'm sure to many parents of a typical teen, the snarky kind who closes herself in her room and ignores her parents, this sounds like heaven. But honestly, as wonderful as it is to have a kid who is her own person, it does worry me, just a teensy bit, that she's not going through the normal growing-up channels. And because I am an over-anxious ball of crazy, I worry that she'll wait to kiss her first boy and drink her first beer until she's off on her own, at college, without the safety net of home to catch her. See, one person's heaven is another's cause for concern. And no matter what our kids do, it seems like we can always find something to obsess over.

TINA. There ought to be a pill developed for that moment right after you find out your daughter has had sex. When you see the evidence – when there's no doubt about it anymore. There it is. And you need something – ANYTHING – to stop the moment in time, even just temporarily. Something pretty friggin potent. Because let me tell you, coming from a person who had convinced herself she was okay with it when it happened…. I thought I'd girded myself from this reaction through solid preparation. Honest talks? Check! Wisdom imparted? Check! Self-esteem built? Yup! Early action contraception? Yes! And yet, when it was completely without doubt, without question, that she'd done this thing, I was heartbroken. Not mad, not angry, not even surprised. Just sad. Now she's officially herself. Not mine. After years and years of being nearly everything in her life, I am now demoted to being a very important thing in her life. Still loves me, still needs me. But not in the same way. She's the boss of her now. Her body. Her plans. Her turn.

****

ANN. So, I'm out running on a beautiful spring New England day – and I see these two women walking toward me. And I smile, sharing the beauty of the moment with these strangers, but they don't see me, because they're TEXTING. While they're out. With each other, walking. I'm DONE! The whole cell phone, Facebook, Tweet, Twitter, Skype, Bluetooth, IM, texting, sexting, upload, attach, PDF, apps, blog, drop & drag, add to cart emoticon insanity is killing me.

WEN. I'm getting emails from some schmuck from junior high trying to LinkedIn or Friend me, or whatever it is. First of all, sounds sexual, second of all I DON'T KNOW THEM! Didn't want to friend them in 1978, don't want to now.

TINA. I'd like to create a sister business to LinkedIn called Fuck Off.

JANE. The other night I see my kid sitting NEXT to her friend on the couch, and they're texting, instead of TALKING.

TINA. This morning at 6 o'clock my cell phone starts ringing AND vibrating…

WEN. …again, sexual!

TINA. …I figure someone's dead. But no, it's the Superintendent of Schools with the 27th automated school health update.

JANE. And I don't know about your kids, but what about making an old fashioned phone call? "But Mom, how do I let Mrs. Sullivan know I can't babysit on Saturday?" Well honey, we have these crazy communication devices where you can talk voice to voice with her. "But I don't know her phone number?" Are you kidding me?

ANN. Same with their friends. The idea of my daughter picking up a phone to ask a friend over – it's like I'm from Mars if I suggest it. "Mom, I sent her a text!" Woudn't it be nice if they could just be girlfriends on a couch using their eyes, and words and hearts to communicate?

WEN. No such thing as actually going over to someone's house and interacting human to human. That's gone. Old School.

ANN. What about the taking selfies non stop.

JANE. Posting every emotion online.

TINA. Song lyrics have never been quoted more.

ANN. I try to limit their time on the laptops, Playstation, iPad, TV, but it is a war most of the time.

WEN. I've given up and raised the white flag. Surrendered. It's the way they interact with their friends now.

ANN. The social interaction thing is only happening in cyber space. SCARY.

JANE. At least at home, they are semi-forced to interact with my husband and me. And their brother and sister. Although that brings us back to war.

ANN. Yeah - talk about your love-hate relationship. My son and daughter.

TINA. Or sisters and sisters – WHOA. Intense.

WEN. Yeah, I thought navigating the minefield of college roommates was something. Or just growing up the youngest of four. But watching it from the other side – watching your kids battle it out on a daily, hourly basis is another thing entirely.

ANN. I love it when I can overhear them, talking and planning and working together in the way every parent secretly hopes for. They're collaborating on some game, some project, hatching elaborate schemes and storylines – they're both pretty prolific bullshitters. They don't know I'm behind the door, and so they continue their game, sharing and compromising and I totally have to keep my smile from bursting through.

WEN. Yeah, because most of the time my kids are in the same vicinity, it seems to be loud and angry, he's pushing her every button and she's screaming back and hurling the most hurtful insults.

TINA. Civil war. Opposing sides. You're Lincoln trying to hold the Union together.

ANN. And all you are thinking is why, why did I have more than one kid?? What was I thinking?? They HATE each other.

WEN. But then you catch them cooperating, collaborating even and you remember why you have more than one. And even though it is only a fraction of the time they spend together, it is somehow enough.

JANE. At least I hope they are confiding things to each other that they wouldn't confide in me. You know, the same topics we avoided talking to our parents about?

ANN. Like, how do you find time to have sex with your spouse?

TINA. You mean "Oh, we're so busy, how do we sandwich it in between work, PTO meetings and driver's ed?"

TINA. No, I mean how do you find time when you have teens in the house? It's not like when they were little and you could set them up with cereal and cartoons and sneak away to the bedroom for some and no one would be the wiser.

WEN. Or could "take a nap" when they did. I know what you mean…

ANN. I love that they get all that sex ed in school, but now they KNOW what people are doing behind closed doors!

JANE. And it's embarrassing as hell to sneak off without being noticed, lock the door, be quiet as mice…

ANN. Because THAT'S so easy…

TINA. Only to hear, as soon as you're at that really critical moment, of course, "Mom? Mom, where are you?? I need my jacket, my saxophone, money, a ride (fill in the blank)!"

WEN. Ooh, have you tried doing it in the laundry room? My kids NEVER go in there!

JANE. Well, forget bedtime; my kids stay up way later than I do. I used to be such a night owl, but between their youth and unending homework, I just can't outlast them.

ANN. I try, but even if I do manage to say goodnight and then shut off ALL the lights I find my husband snoring away, out like a light. Which I'm actually kind of grateful for, because by that time I'm pretty exhausted myself, and the idea of getting revved up for sex is, well, daunting.

TINA. Huh, maybe this is why menopause coincides with their teen years.

****

ANN. Having kids is like a marriage – or any good relationship. In the beginning, everything is so cute and adorable and funny. Then as time goes on, and you spend more time together and you get to know all the intimate things about them, good and bad, the bloom is off the rose. The rose colored glasses are gone. Pretty soon you are taking them for granted, and wondering about other kids who would be really great to have as your own, and needing some time apart. It's God's way of helping you let go. They start to annoy the hell out of you so you don't coddle them so much. And so you won't miss them too much when they are gone. Ok, well that part is probably not going to happen. So, yeah, the relationship goes through all the stages that any long term commitment does. Only this one ends with a large tuition bill.

WEN. Who knew that so much of the college application process would be just like The Hunger Games? It's all there, the randomness of who gets picked, the hysterical parents trying not to be too involved since it doesn't do any good, the makeovers and training so that your candidate is presentable and of course, the ruthless fight to the finish. Okay, it's not so bad and of course everyone will get into the right school for them, and whatever was meant to be, blah, blah, blah. And yeah, in my house we all tried hard not to give into the craziness and be zen. But still, so glad that phase is over. And I'll be much better prepared for the next kid who enters the arena.

JANE. So, I'm visiting colleges with my oldest daughter and she is one of those kids who wants to do it all herself. *(hold hand out in the 'stop' signal)* "I Got This, Mom." She doesn't want any hand holding – at all – from her father and me. But she still needs us – to transport her to the schools for visits, to gently guide her without really saying anything because any suggestion from us is the Kiss. Of. Death. – and of course, to spend our money to underwrite these visits and all the rest of it. And I know that even though she doesn't let on, NOT AT ALL, she's glad we are going with her. Truly. So for this reason, and sooo many others, it seems to me that 90% of parenting a teenager is three things: Show up. Shut up. Pay up. Like teaching them how to drive. Get in the passenger seat. DO NOT SAY A WORD. Pay for the privilege of being scared out of your f%$@@% mind either while driving with them – where my face basically is frozen into a re-creation of Munch's *(pronounced "Monk")* The Scream – or panicking at home while they are out driving around. Or show up at the football game where they are in Pep Band. Do not talk to them. Try and act invisible. Convince yourself that they are glad you are there anyway. If you want their attention, just hold up a $5 bill that they will grab on their way to the concession stand, and if you are very lucky, they will use manners since they are out in public and of course the world gets the best part of them. Whatever you do, don't try and say hi to them or chat with their friends – just *Give up the Money*. Show up, Shut up. Pay up. Your guide to the teenage years.

****

TINA. For all the bitching and moaning we do, there's no question I am ridiculously blessed. We all are. Our kids are healthy and thriving and sure there are issues, and mistakes being made on all sides, but hey, that's life, right?

ANN. It's hard to believe we've been parenting for 17 years and counting at this point. It's like – wow, we've almost done it, we've almost made it.

JANE. It really has gone by in the blink of an eye. The whole 'days are long but years are short' thing.

WEN. And so much has changed, especially in the past few years. But there is so much that's EXACTLY THE SAME.

JANE. Yeah, you mean like the stuff we say over and over?

ANN. 'If you can't say something nice…'

TINA. When you have kids of your own, you'll understand.

ANN. I'm not going to ask you again.

TINA. Don't make me stop this car?

JANE. Serves you right.

WEN. Are you going out dressed like that?

ANN. Skirt down to your fingertips.

TINA. Shirt's too tight. Uh, uh, uh.

Put a different shirt on before your father gets home.

ANN. Back upstairs and try again.

JANE. Nope, still no good

JANE. Collared shirt for this. No t-shirts.

WEN. It's 30 degrees – what about a coat?

ANN. Shorts – in winter?

JANE. Make good choices!

ANN. Be good!

TINA. Remember your manners! Remember manners?

JANE. Yes it is fair.

ANN. Well, sometimes life isn't fair.

TINA. Cry me a river.

WEN. Tough.

ANN. Tough shit.

WEN. Yes I did swear. Get over it.

JANE. Look at me when I'm talking to you.

ANN. Don't you roll your eyes at me.

TINA. That's enough sass from you, young lady.

JANE. If you want to go swimming, wear a tampon.

ANN. Just keep pushing it in.

TINA. It happens. Just try and find the string.

WEN. When was the last time you took a shower? Seriously.

TINA. Time is UP in the shower.

WEN. Get out of the shower.

JANE. You're taking a shower again?

WEN. What the hell are you doing in there? … Don't answer that (*say under your breath-ish*)

ANN. Okay, enough with the AXE.

WEN. Homework is a fact of life.

ANN. Is your homework done?

JANE. ALL your homework?

ANN. Stop texting while I'm talking to you.

WEN. Your friends can wait.

JANE. Deal with it.

ANN. Vacation's over. So over.

TINA. It'll be fun to see all your friends at school again!

JANE. DON'T YELL AT YOUR BROTHER LIKE THAT!

ANN. Is your life really so hard?

JANE. I AM NOT YOUR SERVANT!

ANN. I AM NOT THE MAID!

TINA. Did you feed the dogs?

WEN. The Guinea pig?

JANE. CAN SOMEONE PLEASE REPLACE THE TOILET PAPER ROLL?

ANN. IS IT REALLY THAT HARD TO TAKE OUT THE GARBAGE?

ANN. I didn't ask who put it there, I said "Pick it up!"

JANE. Now, say you're sorry…and MEAN it!

WEN. How do you know you don't like it if you haven't tasted it?

JANE. Screen time is OVER!

ANN. Go outside! It's a beautiful day!

WEN. What is Snapchat?

ANN. Reddit?

JANE. Vine?

TINA. Tumblr?

ANN. When you make the money, buy the groceries, put them away, and cook the meals, you can decide what we eat.

JANE. I don't care if you know kids in 5th grade with an iPhone.

ANN. I am the mean mom. Don't I know it!

WEN. Well I don't hate you.

TINA. As long as you live under my roof, you'll do as I say.

ANN. Do not text and drive. Don't call anyone. Phone PUT AWAY!

JANE. Drive in the right hand lane.

WEN. It's not you I worry about, it's the other drivers.

TINA. Just say you have to go to the bathroom and get out of the car.

ANN. Pretend to be sick. Threaten to throw up.

JANE. Wear your seatbelt!

TINA. Really wear it – not under your arm.

WEN. Text me when you get there.

JANE. Nothing good happens after midnight.

ANN. I don't have to explain myself. I said no.

JANE. Who's going to be at the party?

TINA. Will the parents be home?

WEN. I'm calling the parents… Too bad.

ANN. Want me to call the waaam-bulance?

JANE. You kiss your mother with that mouth?

TINA. I know it's a plant and legal in places. Still makes you stupid.

ANN. Remember – safety first.

JANE. I don't care what "everyone" is doing. I care what YOU are doing!

WEN. Be good – but if you can't be good, be careful.

TINA. Protection is very, very important.

ANN. You should wait. Your father and I did. *(cough, cough)*

ANN. Five minutes of pleasure is not worth a lifetime of hell.

WEN. I'll treat you like an adult when you start acting like one.

ANN. I can't wait until you have kids of your own.

TINA. You're not supposed to like me.

WEN. I just want what's best for you.

JANE. I'm doing this for your own good.

ANN. No one will ever love you like I will.

TINA. And don't you forget it.

****

ANN. I lost my mother. Doesn't that sound so much better than saying she died?? It makes it sound like we went to the mall and somehow got separated, and if I just wait long enough, she'll turn up. But of course, that won't really happen. And the really shitty part of losing your mother is all the other things you lose: access to free medical advice, someone who can tell you exactly how you SHOULD wear your hair, her famous raisin bread at Thanksgiving. And a million other things that drove me crazy. And it really doesn't matter how old you get, or how many other small people are demanding the same from you, you still really need that one person who knows you to your core, who sat up with you all night when you had the croup, who listened to you cry inconsolably over your first heartbreak, who told you everything would be ok and then hung up the phone and fretted over you. Who loved you and your offspring to the depths of her being. No matter what. And even scarier, now I'M The Mom; there is no greater power above me that I can reference. Now I have to be the expert, the one who knows how to check for swollen glands, the top mom in the food chain. I just hope I'm up to the challenge…

TINA. My uterus has served me well. Honest to God. Three amazing daughters formed in that womb. As guys say about old cars, it doesn't owe me anything. But now things are different. The old…sorry!…original uterus is all done. Ship sailed. Horse left barn. But the need for such a womb continues. Because yeah, the cells have split and developed. The DNA is formed and the dominant features determined. But that is only the beginning of creating a person: there's a lot that goes on after delivery. So now I've created a virtual womb. It's purpose? Get my kids though the next phases of development. There's the little stuff, like how to drive in snow, navigate a map, floss. How to get over a heinous haircut, and the ins and outs of zits and when to squeeze. But there's the big stuff, too. How to deal with mean, small-minded girls who exclude them from the after school trip. How to fathom death the first time it comes close to them. How to laugh at themselves, and show kindness to those less blessed. How to honor their bodies and minds, avoid addictions and fight the downward spiral of self-loathing. How to love themselves enough to be ready to love someone else. Yeah, I know there are babies born every minute, and it's easy to chalk it up to just another face showing up on the planet. But when it happens to you – when that new creature is yours, when your cynicism and world weariness are knocked to their knees with a wall of awe, that new face is nothing short of the truest and most timeless love of all. When they thrive, you celebrate. When they succeed, you beam. And when they need you – at 3, or 15 or 27, you run to them. The forever womb.

WEN. My oldest is a senior. She is so ready to go out in the world and I think I'm ready too. Okay, sure, no one is going to accuse me of being a low-key mom all these years, and I'm as guilty as the next of overinvolvement on a lot of levels. But in a whole other way, my daughter has taught me that she is capable and confident and that it's really okay that I let her to find her way. On her own in the truest sense. Without her father and me. Making decisions. Navigating problems and choices. Learning without us. Guiding herself. As moms we try and teach our kids – every day, every minute – we are mentors, therapists, dictators even. But you know what? They teach us too. Sometimes more than we will ever teach them. They show us the way, how to *be*, and they do it in a way that is uniquely, amazingly, their own. So, when it's time to drop my daughter off, I know it will be hard, and I know I will try to be strong and I might fail, and she might – will – fail too as she goes on. But she has shown me that she is ready to take on the world. And I can't wait to know about the next chapter of her life.

TINA. Our job is to raise our kids so we can let them go. A wise mom told me that once and I always try to remember that. The connection between us – that starts with the umbilical cord or just the first time we hold them in our arms – however they got there – will always be there no matter what. But if we've done our job right, if we accept that they need to go out in the world, and make their own way, their own mistakes, their own life, with us on the sidelines, if we make peace with that, then maybe, just maybe, we can have a moment of feeling of the job well done. Yeah, sure, there will always be areas where we want a do-over. Moments in time that got away from us, regrets over the significant and trivial mistakes we made. Connections with our children that we dreamed about that didn't happen. Directions they go in that veer off from what we envisioned. But the magic of it all is that we have gotten to be in relationship with our children whose indelible imprint on our lives colors and shades everything else in it. Although it doesn't feel like it every day, it is the most powerful gift we can receive. The gift of loving and being loved by extraordinary people, who just happen to be our children. Forever grateful, forever a mom even when they leave the nest, on to their next adventure.

****